Best
Little
House

Best Little House

BY

AILEEN FISHER

ILLUSTRATED BY

ARNOLD SPILKA

Thomas Y. Crowell Company

NEW YORK

By the Author

GOING BAREFOOT
WHERE DOES EVERYONE GO?
LIKE NOTHING AT ALL
I LIKE WEATHER
LISTEN, RABBIT
IN THE MIDDLE OF THE NIGHT
BEST LITTLE HOUSE

Best
Little
House

I said good-bye
to the grass and trees
and the places I'd crawled
on my hands and knees
under the lilacs
cool and green
where I couldn't be seen . . .

I said good-bye
to the fence and gate
and the garden chair
that had lost its mate
and the hole near the hedge
where I dug for gold
when I was only
just-four-years-old.

I watched an ant
crawl over a plant
where a streak of sun
came down on a slant,
and I said good-bye
with a blink of my eye.

I went indoors
and I walked around,
and the floors made an empty
walked-on sound
with the rugs rolled up,
and the walls looked bare
without any pictures
hanging there.
And the furniture
wasn't like ours at all,
pushed around
and away from the wall,
ready to move on the van
that day.

But *I* wasn't ready
to move away.

I said good-bye . . .
and my throat felt tight
so I rushed upstairs
and out of sight.

I lay on my bed
that was stripped and bare
and wondered why parents
didn't care
if they moved away
(like Mother and Dad),
after such fun
in the house they had.

I thought I never
had felt so bad.

Way out there
at the edge of town
there wouldn't be houses
up and down.
Who would I know?
How would I play?
Why did *anyone* move away?

I saw my music box
on the shelf
and thought:

"I'll carry it myself
so when we live
at the edge of town
I'll have *one* friend
when the rain comes down,
and a song to play
on a lonesome day."

Under the gaily painted towers
hidden inside, away,
in the fancy box
with the dancy flowers,
the music-makers stay:

Toot-toot-toot
goes a little gold flute.

Out and in
weaves a violin.

Tum-tum-tum
goes a faraway drum
when the music-makers play.

I tinkled a tune
and said good-bye
to my window
holding a piece of sky
and the tree looking in
that had grown so high.

And then we moved
to the edge of town
where hardly a house
showed up or down.
And I went to bed,
and my room was blue
(instead of yellow)
and I was, too.

To keep sad dreams
from filling my head,
I put my music box
on my bed,
and the music-makers
who lived inside
played me to sleep . . .
or at least they tried.

I closed my eyes
and what a surprise!

As the little gold flute
went toot–toot–toot
I fell through the sky
in a parachute!

I landed in places
I never had been
to the tune of the music-box
violin.

And oh, it was very
adventuresome
to walk among houses
as small as my thumb,
as tall as castles
in Kingdom Come,
while the music-box drum
went tum–tum–tum.

Then all of a sudden
beside my bed
my mother was standing
with sun on her head,
winding the music box
as she said:
"Time to get up.
There's honey and bread
and melon for breakfast."

I raised my head.

Toot-toot-toot
went the little gold flute.

Tum-tum-tum
went the music-box drum.

Out and in
wove the violin . . .

As I told my mother
where I had been:

Where magical houses
showed up and down,
not just US
at the edge of town.

My mother's eyes
had a twinkly gleam.
"Houses?" she said.
"You couldn't *dream*
how many I've found
right close around."

Her voice made a chuckly
sort of sound.
"Magical houses!
Take your flute
and we'll go on a tour
with a toot-toot-toot."

We slipped through the door
and across the floor
and down the stairs
past tables and chairs
and out to the yard
where the sun shone hard
to the toot-toot-toot
of my little toy flute.

And soon my mother
held up her hand
and said, "Don't step
on that house of sand."

House of SAND?

She pointed down
to a tiny funnel,
not like a cave,
not like a tunnel,
and said, "Down there
with the roof caved in
an ant lion waits
with sand in his skin
and sand on the hairs
of his chinny-chin-chin,
ready to pounce
if an ant falls in."

A *lion*?

"He's shorter
than half a pin."

So I called, "Hello,"
and tooted a song,
and we flute-flute-
fluted along.

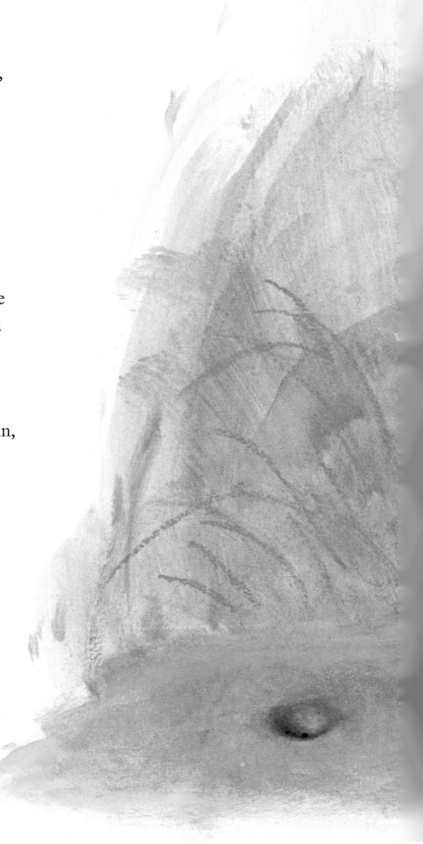

We hurried ahead
with a skip and caper,
and soon Mom said:
"There's a house of paper."

A house of PAPER?

Hanging there
from a busy bracket
was the house of a hornet
or yellow jacket,
a house full of rooms
like seeds in a packet.

"Don't ask me *how*,
but the hornets know
the papery way
their walls should go,"
my mother said
as she cocked her head,
"and layer by layer
they build them so."

We didn't go close,
just waved Hello,
and once again I began to play
and we toot-toot-tooted away.

Then in a second
my mother beckoned
and said she reckoned
a house of mud
lay close to a bud.

A house of MUD?

"A neat little jug
of mud and clay,"
she said with a shrug
in a knowing way,
"is dry and snug
on a chilly day
for the egg that a wasp
has stored away . . .

a potter wasp
who neatly attaches
the house to a leaf
in weedy patches,
with food inside
which the baby snatches
as soon as it hatches."

"Hello," I said,
"in your house of clay."
And we flute-toot-tooted away.

We stopped in front
of a Woodpecker Tree.

"It's full of neighbors
as it can be,"
my mother leaned over
and said to me,
"for a hole is a house
of the nicest kind
and very much in demand,
you'll find."

A HOLE is a house?

"A hole," said she,
"makes a homey room
though it hasn't a key
or a plant in bloom
or a stove or broom
or a cup of tea
or a kettle or crock
or a door to knock
or a clock to tock
tick-tock-tick-tock.

"A hole is a house
for a white-footed mouse
who scampers about
when the stars are out
and the moon is a light
for the hills of night.

"A hole in a tree,"
she said to me,
"is a very fine house
for a chickadee
who has the habit
of lining her nest
from east to west
with the fluff of a rabbit.

"It all depends
on the size of the hollow,"
my mother said.
"Does it fit a swallow?
A possum?
A bee?
Or a masked raccoon
who likes to roam
by the light of the moon
and likes to rest
with a hole for a nest
in a tree by day,
all hidden away?"

"What a magical place
a hole can be,"
I said with a bow
to the Woodpecker Tree.

And we toot-toot-tooted
along our way
until my mother
stopped short to say:
"Forget your worries,
forget your troubles . . .
they're made of froth
like a house of bubbles."

A house of BUBBLES?

There on a bush
shone blobs of froth,
cooler than sand,
cooler than cloth,
where frog-hoppers lived
(not frogs at all,
but insects timid
and queer and small),
sitting inside
a frothy bubble,
trying to hide,
with their knees bent double.

"Hello," I said
to the frog-hopper folk
who didn't go hopping
and didn't croak
like frogs in a bog,
but merely sat
in houses of fog
to be wondered at.

We tooted on,
past the sweeping eaves
of a spruce, to a birch's
spangled leaves,
and Mom said, "Look!
Here's a house of leaves."

A house of LEAVES?

On a leafy branch
in a shady place
hung a house of green
in a rolled-up case,
a leafy house
that an insect made
to hide the cluster
of eggs she laid.

"There's a leaf-roller moth,
and a leaf-cutter bee,
and a beetle preferring
a birchwood tree,"
my mother stopped
to explain to me.
"But I don't know which
made the house you see."

"It's quite," I said,
my flute in my hand,
"as strange
as the music-makers' land."

A house of sand,
of paper,
of clay,
a hole for a house
by night or day,
a house of bubbles,
of leaves . . . What *next*?
I wondered,
and tooted off, perplexed.

"A house of silk,"
my mother called out,
as if she heard
what I wondered about.

A house of SILK?

I knew cocoons
were houses of silk,
brown or tan
or the color of milk,
where somebody lived
who soon would try
to open her wings
and flutter and fly,
light as a breeze
in the bright blue sky . . .
and oh, I wished
I had wings to try.

Then all of a sudden
we heard some cries,
and Father was calling
and sounding wise:
"Here's a house," he called,
"that's a big surprise."

"A house?" I laughed.
And I asked my mother
if there could possibly
be another.

"You never can tell
what your Dad will do,"
she said with a wink,
so I knew she *knew*.

"Hurry!" cried Father,
and waved from the shed.

"Scurry!" said Mother
and nodded her head.

So I went in a flurry,
and here's what they said:

"We both of us thought
till the place built up
you'd rattle around
like an old tin cup,
so we bought you a house . . .
a house for a pup."

A house for a PUP?

"A house for a pup
is best," I cried.
"*Especially best*
for what's inside!"

For there inside
on a bed of hay
a not-very-big
little puppy lay,
waiting for someone
to come and play
and rollick and frolic
from bush to tree . . .
waiting for someone
who looked like ME.

About the Author

AILEEN FISHER'S "Best Little House" is the cabin where she lives on a ranch in the foothills of Colorado—a cabin which she helped build with her own hands. From the window at her desk she looks beyond pasture and pine-covered hills to Arapahoe Peak.

Miss Fisher was born on the Upper Peninsula of Michigan. When she was five, her family moved to a farm near Iron River, and it was there that she learned to love the outdoors and to look forward to the changing seasons. Her first poetry was written for the high school column in the local newspaper. Since that time she has written many books and plays for children. She attended the University of Chicago and later received a degree in journalism from the University of Missouri.

About the Illustrator

ARNOLD SPILKA has illustrated many delightful books for children, and his drawings perfectly match the mood of Aileen Fisher's lilting verse for *Best Little House*.

Mr. Spilka was born in New York City, and he studied at the Art Students' League. He has also studied drawing with Rico Lebrun and sculpture with John Hovannes. Mr. Spilka has traveled in Belgium, England, France, and Luxembourg; he lives in New York.